THIS WALKER BOOK BELONGS TO:

_____

_____

_____

To Tereza and Cecilia with lots of love

First published 2003 by Walker Books Ltd
87 Vauxhall Walk, London SE11 5HJ

This edition published 2005

10 9 8 7 6 5 4 3 2 1

© 2003 Petr Horáček

The right of Petr Horáček to be identified as author/illustrator
of this work has been asserted by him in accordance with the
Copyright, Designs and Patents Act 1988

WB Horáček font © 2003 Petr Horáček

Printed in China

British Library Cataloguing in Publication Data:
a catalogue record for this book is available from the British Library

ISBN 0-7445-7047-6

www.walkerbooks.co.uk

WALKER BOOKS
AND SUBSIDIARIES
LONDON · BOSTON · SYDNEY · AUCKLAND

When the Moon Smiled

Petr Horáček

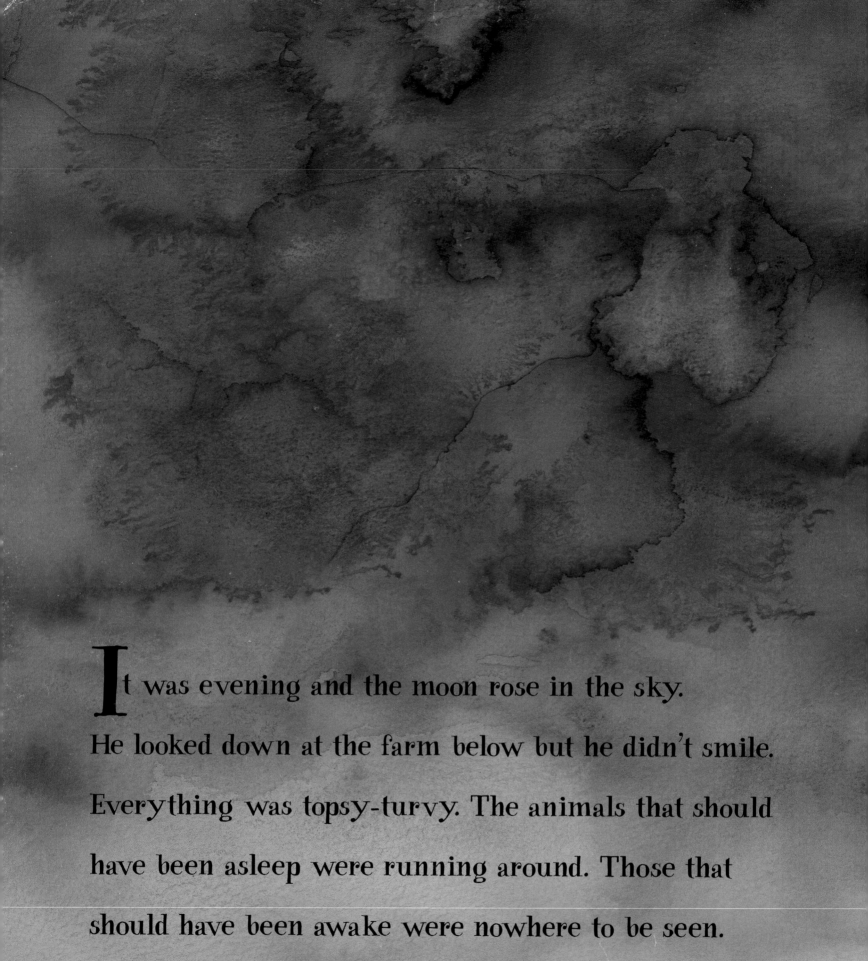

It was evening and the moon rose in the sky.

He looked down at the farm below but he didn't smile.

Everything was topsy-turvy. The animals that should

have been asleep were running around. Those that

should have been awake were nowhere to be seen.

"I must put things right," said the moon. "It's time to light the stars."

So the moon lit the first star. "This is for the dog,"

he said, and the dog yawned and went to sleep.

The moon lit the second star. "For the cats," he said,

and the cats stretched and went out for a prowl.

"The third star is for the cows," said the moon,

and the cows settled down and closed their eyes.

"The fourth star is for the bats," said the moon,

and the bats left the barn and fluttered into the night.

"The fifth star is for the pigs," said the moon,

and the pigs lay down in the squelchy mud.

"The sixth star is for the foxes," said the moon,

and the foxes sniffed the air ready to hunt.

As the moon lit the seventh star, the geese stopped

honking. Things were becoming quieter.

"The eighth star is for the mice," said the moon,

and the mice woke up and scurried in the hay.

"The ninth star is for the sheep," said the moon,

and the sheep curled up and were quiet.

"The tenth star is for the moths," said the moon,

and the moths danced in the night sky.

At last the sky was full of stars shining above the farm.

"That's better," said the moon, and then he smiled.

WALKER BOOKS is the world's leading
independent publisher of children's books.
Working with the best authors and illustrators
we create books for all ages, from babies
to teenagers – books your child will
grow up with and always remember. So…

FOR THE BEST CHILDREN'S BOOKS,
LOOK FOR THE BEAR